The Day it Rained
Letters

By Nury Vittachi

Illustrated by Eamonn O'Boyle

H hachette
INDIA

First published in India in 2009 by Hachette India
An Hachette UK Company
First published by PPP Company Limited, 2005

Copyright © 2005 PPP Company Limited, original text: Nury Vittachi,
illustrations: Eamonn O'Boyle. The original text by Nury Vittachi is published
with the kind permission of Chameleon Press Limited.

ISBN: 978-93-80143-05-7

For sale in the Indian Subcontinent only

Hachette India
612/614 (6th Floor), Time Tower
MG Road, Sector 28, Gurgaon-122001, India

Typeset in Goudy Old Style
by PPP Company Ltd., Hong Kong

Printed in India by Gopsons Papers Ltd., Noida

Dedicated to Christina Noble

All author's royalties from this edition of *The Day it Rained Letters* are being donated to the Christina Noble Children's Foundation

Once upon a time,
there was a land with
no storybooks.

Not even this one.

5

The shelf in Minky Binka's room had no books, only junk.

At bedtime, children all over the land looked at their moms and dads, and their moms and dads looked at them – but there were no bedtime stories to tell. So parents just said: 'Goodnight,' and turned off the lights.

At her school, there was no story time, only lessons. No storybooks meant no imagination, so at playtime no one played any games. They just waited.

7

There was even an old printing house on the edge of town, but it made no books, only empty cardboard boxes.

The land without stories was a quiet and boring place.

One day, Minky Binka was walking through a park
on the way to school, when she saw a cloud that
looked like a person's head – it really did. It had a
face and a nose and big chubby cheeks. A tiny spark
of imagination fizzed inside her brain.

'Hello, cloud,' she said.

Something fell on her head.

'Ouch!' said Minky Binka. But
she was not really hurt, just
surprised. Whatever had landed
on her head, fell from her hair
to the floor. She picked it up. It
was small and flat and circular.
She put it in her pocket and
forgot all about it.

She forgot all about it, that is, until the
next day. She was walking through the
park again, and another something fell on
her head. Again, she picked it up.
This time it was small and flat and sort of
cross-shaped. She put it in her pocket.

11

That evening, Minky Binka showed her
mother the shapes.

'What are these things, Mother Dear?'
Minky Binka asked.

Minky Binka's Mother Dear picked
them up. 'I don't know,' she said. 'Where
did you find them?'

'They fell out of the sky,' Minky Binka said. 'And landed – *donk!* – on my head.'

Mother Dear couldn't think what they could be. She said she was tired because she had been looking at screens all day in the office and wanted to relax. So she sat in front of the television.

Minky Binka put the pretty shapes in her treasure box along with her favourite ribbon and a seashell with stripes on it.

The next day, Minky Binka took the shapes to school and held them up during show-and-tell.

'I don't know what these are,' she said. 'But they fell on my head.'

At playtime, when all the children were standing around, not playing but waiting, a boy called Rama Khan came to see her. He held up a shape similar to Minky Binka's but different.

'This fell out of the sky onto my head,' he said. 'It's a bit like yours.'

Minky Binka and Rama Khan
went to the park after school
every day to look for more
shapes. They found three
more – two in the grass and
one on the path.

On Saturday, Mother Dear took Minky Binka to the library to see if they could learn anything about the shapes.

In the library of the land with no storybooks, there were no storybooks. But there was a librarian and rows and rows of wise old people.

'We want to find out about these shapes,' Mother Dear said to the librarian.

The librarian looked at them carefully. She said: 'They're interesting shapes. I wonder if they have meanings?'

'Go and see old Mr. Reed, our encyclopaedia. He's in row twelve, seat four,' she said.

17

Old Mr. Reed carefully examined Minky Binka's shapes. 'Goodness me!' he said. 'You've found some letters of the alphabet. These are very rare, very rare indeed.'

He told them that the shapes used to be common and were once used to make up stories.

'What's a story?' Minky Binka asked. 'And what does "make up" mean?'

Mr. Reed said it was hard to explain. 'Stories were wonderful, enjoyable, scrumptious things,' he said. 'In the old days, they were served on thin plates called pages. You ate them with your eyes.'

Minky Binka was amazed. 'You ate them with your eyes?' she asked. 'That is so weird.'

'And they didn't go down to your tummy, like normal food,' Mr. Reed said. 'No, they went into a dream machine inside your head.'

'Oh,' said the girl. 'And did the dream machine make dreams?'

Mr. Reed thought about this for a moment. 'If I remember rightly, it did much more than that. The more stories went into the dream machine, the more imagination came out. Imagination was wonderful stuff. I wish we still had it.'

Mother Dear asked:
'What is Imagination?'

'That's also hard to explain,' Mr. Reed said. 'Imagination gives children the ability to dream dreams even when they are awake. It gives them the ability to have exciting, dangerous adventures without any danger. It gives them the power to turn themselves into pirates or princesses or porcupines. With Imagination, children can fly around the world, travel through space, or even go forwards and backwards in time. And they can do all this without leaving their chairs.'

Minky Binka was amazed. Imagination must be a wonderful thing to have. She stared at the shapes in front of her. 'I'm going to eat these with my eyes,' she said.

Mr. Reed laughed. 'I'm afraid you can't. If you just have one or two or even twenty, it doesn't work. You have to have a great many for the system to work.'

'Fifty?' she asked.

'More,' he said.

'A hundred?'

'More.'

'A thousand?'

'More.'

'Ten thousand?'

Mr. Reed nodded: 'Yes. I think ten thousand would be a good number.'

Minky Binka was disappointed. 'We've only got six. Where can I get ten thousand little shapes?'

The old man shook his head. 'I don't know. In the old days, they were everywhere. But when films became more and more common, storybooks disappeared – and Imagination went with them.'

On Saturday afternoon, Minky Binka met her friend Rama Khan and they went to the park to look for shapes. 'If we find nine thousand nine hundred and ninety-four more of them, we can eat them with our eyes,' she explained. 'That will make the dream machines in our heads start working.'

'Eat them with our eyes?' said Rama Khan. 'That is so weird.'

They searched all over the park. They went down on their knees in the grass. They climbed trees to look at the branches. They fished with nets in the pond.

By the end of the day, they had found seven more letters. They still had nine thousand nine hundred and eighty-seven more to find.

It was getting dark so they gave up the search and headed home.

As they walked through the town square, a wind began to blow. The clouds blew away to reveal a starry sky and a glowing blue moon.

'The moon's like a magic lantern tonight,' said Rama Khan.

Minky Binka nodded. 'Yes,' she said. 'I think it's God's night-light.'

Something fell on Minky Binka's head. 'Another one!' she said, pulling a letter out of her hair.

'I've got one too,' said Rama Khan, clutching one out of the air with his hand. 'It's raining magic tonight.'

'Where are they coming from?' Minky Binka asked. 'Someone up there's dropping them on us.'

As they looked up, they saw more letters falling from the sky, like tiny snowflakes.

'I'll catch those,' she said, running to scoop them from the air.

'And I'll get the others,' said Rama Khan, running in the other direction.

More letters fell, and more, and more. Soon, there were hundreds of them. They drifted through the air like snow and got caught in people's hair and clothes. They landed on the ground and began to cover the pavements.

Minky Binka and Rama Khan danced around, scooping them up and showering them over each other.

The blizzard of letters was still going on when it was time for Minky Binka and Rama Khan to go home.

That night, Minky Binka was too excited to sleep. She got out of bed and ran to the window. Opening the curtains, she saw flurries of letters still swirling in the sky.

'By the morning there might be enough,' she said to herself. 'Maybe ten thousand.'

As the sun rose the next day, people looked out of their windows and saw that the deluge of letters had come to an end. The sky was clear. Shapes covered the pavements and were piled up in drifts by the walls.

Minky Binka raced to the library, scattering letters as she ran, to ask Mr. Reed what to do next.

But he was not there. She went to the librarian's desk and asked where he was.

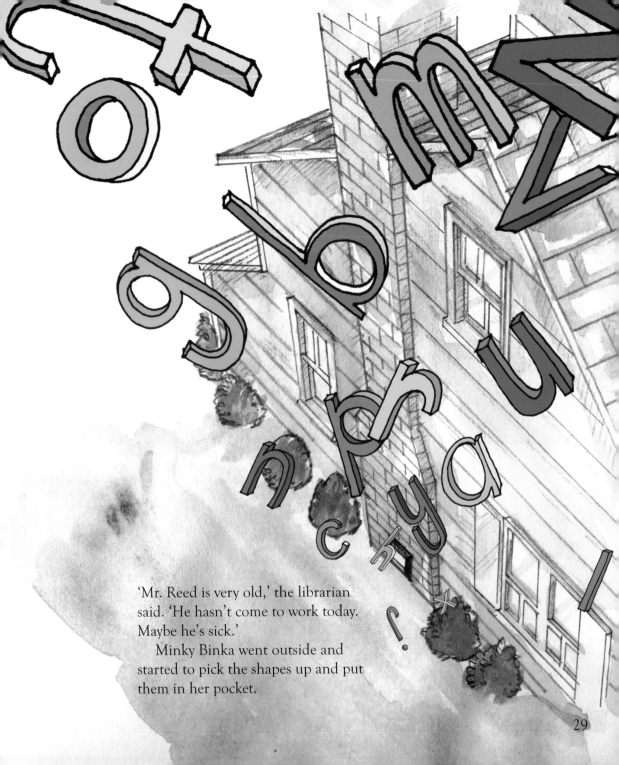

'Mr. Reed is very old,' the librarian said. 'He hasn't come to work today. Maybe he's sick.'

Minky Binka went outside and started to pick the shapes up and put them in her pocket.

29

But around her, she noticed that people were starting to complain about the mess. They said the letters were untidy and troublesome. The chimney sweep said they had fallen into the chimneys.

The plumber said they were blocking the drains.

The Mayor suggested they organize a big bonfire to burn them all.

Minky Binka was alarmed. She was too shy to say anything to the Mayor, so she ran home to Mother Dear.

31

'Let's go to the old printing house on the edge of town, Mother Dear,' said Minky Binka. 'Maybe they'll know what to do with the letters.'

They walked up the hill and found the old building. The factory boss, Bill Hill, said that the storybook printing machine was still there, but it was covered in dust and hadn't been used for many years.

He took them to a walkway over a huge machine which had big rolls of paper and lots of conveyor belts.

Bill Hill turned the switch on, but nothing happened. He pressed some buttons. Still nothing happened. 'I think it doesn't work,' he said.

Then they
heard something
click in the machine
below them. Lights
started to flash. The machine
began to hum.

Bill Hill smiled. 'Maybe it does
work, after all,' he said. 'It was just slow
getting started.'

The machine started chugging and making a
whirring noise. 'Hooray!' said Minky Binka.
The whirring and buzzing noises suggested that
something was being put together. After eight
minutes, a big squarish thing came out and was
carried to them by a conveyor belt. It looked like
a flat brick.

'What is that?' Minky Binka asked.

Bill Hill carefully picked it up. His eyes were big as he stared at it. 'It's a storybook,' he said in a hushed voice. 'I've heard about these. My grandfather used to talk about them. But I've never seen one. This is the first storybook that this land has seen for many, many years.'

He handed it to the young girl. 'It's yours,' he said.

Minky Binka opened it. The pages were blank.

'It doesn't work,' she said. 'I'm looking at the plates, but there's nothing for my eyes to eat.'

35

Just then, they heard a knocking at the door. 'Minky Binka, are you in there?' a voice said.

They opened the door and Rama Khan came running in. 'The letters are all rushing around in the wind. You should see them. This may sound crazy, but... I think they're following me.'

As he finished talking, a flurry of letters zoomed over his head and entered the room. He ducked. They flew to the white pages of the book Minky Binka was holding and laid themselves flat into it.

At the same time, a tinkling sound came from the windows. Tiny shapes were crashing into the windows, trying to get in. Bill Hill opened the factory windows. Letters flooded in from outside, and flew through the air in a mad rush to get into the book.

They watched as the pages flew open as fast as they could, and the letters laid themselves into the book in long, straight lines.

Then, as suddenly as it had started, the storm of letters stopped.

Minky Binka walked to the door of the factory carrying the book.

As she stepped onto the front steps, she was surprised to discover that all the people of the town were waiting outside. They had seen the letters rush into the building and had followed them. The ground was clear again. It seemed that every letter that had fallen onto the town had been caught up in the book.

Minky Binka held it up. 'I've caught them. The little shapes are all in here. This is called a storybook.'

The Mayor said: 'They are untidy things, and probably dangerous. We must burn that thing in the furnace.'

'No, I want to keep it,' said Minky Binka. 'I'll put it in a glass case in the museum. It's the only storybook in the land.'

'Burn it,' said the Mayor.

'Keep it,' said Minky Binka.

'Burn it.'

'Keep it.'

Someone else spoke. 'Eat it,' an old man's voice said.

Everyone looked around. Mr. Reed came out of the factory building. 'I got up early and came to the factory,' he explained. 'I knew I'd have to do some work on the printing machine to get it working.'

The old man walked over to the top step where Minky Binka stood and he sat down carefully beside her. 'Books are not to be burned. And they are not to be kept in glass boxes in museums. We must eat them with our eyes.'

Minky Binka said: 'Can I eat this one now?'

'Yes,' he said. He took the book out of her hand. 'We can share it. We'll use this to get our dream machines working again. I'll show you how.'

He made everyone sit down on the steps. Then he explained to everyone how a storybook works: 'There are no buttons to press. When your eyes hit the page, the story starts automatically. When you take your eyes off the page, the story stops automatically. When you put your eyes back on the page, the story starts again.'

The people were astonished. Rama Khan put his hand up with a question: 'Where do you put the batteries?'

'It needs no batteries,' said Mr. Reed.

'Where do you plug it in?' asked Minky Binka.

'You don't. It's solar-powered,' said Mr. Reed. 'The sun makes it work. Even the light of a single light bulb is enough to power it.'

The people listened in excited silence. Clearly, a storybook was a wonderful thing.

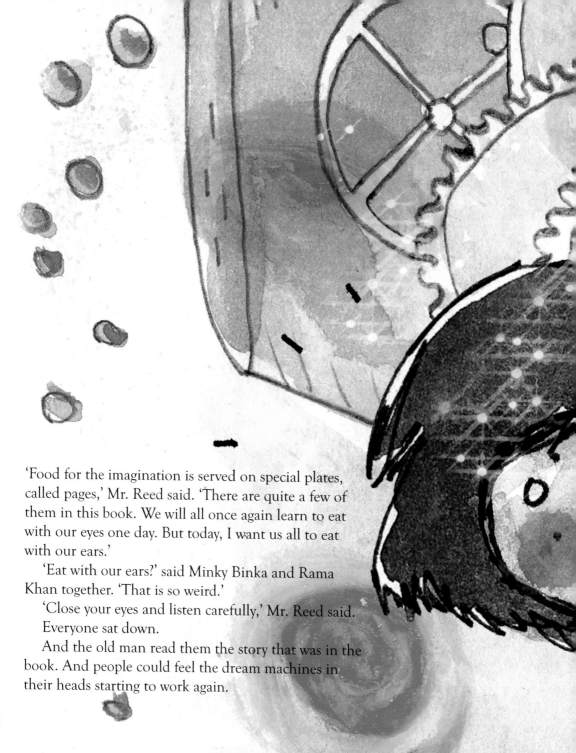

'Food for the imagination is served on special plates, called pages,' Mr. Reed said. 'There are quite a few of them in this book. We will all once again learn to eat with our eyes one day. But today, I want us all to eat with our ears.'

'Eat with our ears?' said Minky Binka and Rama Khan together. 'That is so weird.'

'Close your eyes and listen carefully,' Mr. Reed said. Everyone sat down.

And the old man read them the story that was in the book. And people could feel the dream machines in their heads starting to work again.

44

And this was the story that he told them.
    'Once upon a time, there was a land with no storybooks,' he read. 'Not even this one.'

About the Author and the Illustrator

NURY VITTACHI is one of Asia's best-known writers, the founding editor of the *Asia Literary Review* and chief judge of the Australia-Asia Literary Award. He has published more than 30 books, including the comedy-crime novel series, The Feng Shui Detective. His columns on his website **www.misterjam.com** are read by more than a million people a month. However, his biggest love is children's literature, and he has written many books for them, including *The Paper Princess* and *The True History of Santa Claus*. Vittachi currently lives in Hong Kong with his wife and their three adopted children.

EAMONN O'BOYLE graduated from the National College of Art and Design, Dublin, Ireland. He has been living and working in Hong Kong since then as a freelance illustrator, art director and designer. He has also illustrated a number of children's books, such as *The True History of Santa Claus*, *The Paper Princess* and *The Tales of Ricky*, all published by PPP Company Limited, Hong Kong. He has also contributed to *ABC: Hong Kong's Biggest Alphabet Book*, published in aid of The Child Development Centre.

Samantha's SEA

Written by Angie Belcher
Photographed by Andy Belcher

The author and photographer would like to thank the following organizations for their help in making this book possible:

Air Pacific

Fiji Visitors Bureau

Plantation Island, Fiji

Wananavu Resort, Fiji

Ra Divers, Fiji

Crystal Divers, Fiji

CONTENTS

Inner Space

Introduction

The first time I saw the ocean, I knew I had to sink below its surface and explore its hidden secrets. Never in my wildest dreams did I imagine what bizarre and exotic creatures lived within it. Some of them seemed to be as alien as life on a faraway planet. I guess that's why some people call the ocean "inner space."

If I had been born with gills and a tail, moving and breathing in this watery world would be easy. Instead, I had a lot to learn before I could begin to explore.

First, I had to wait until I was twelve years old, which is the minimum age to get a junior scuba qualification. It took another year to convince my parents that it was something I really wanted to do. Finally, I was able to sign up for a scuba course, which would teach me what I needed to know to delve safely into this underwater world.

"Scuba" stands for self-contained underwater breathing apparatus, and learning how to use it took six weeks of intensive training. My instructor showed me how to assemble my equipment, how to use it, and why each piece was necessary. He helped me understand why staying under water too long and going too deep can be dangerous. I learned about buoyancy and boat handling, floats and flags, entries and exits, rescues and resuscitation. After many hours of studying and plenty of practice in the pool, I finally received my "license to dive."

When I sank below the surface of the sea for the first time, the golden rule of scuba diving pounded through my mind. "Breathe normally; never hold your breath." I was so busy thinking about what to do, I hardly noticed the life around me.

Now, after many dives, I have discovered a whole new world – a world I want to share with you. Come with me on an adventure into inner space.

Secrets of the Sea

Chapter One

With a pounding heart and a babble of bubbles, I am a noisy intruder in this silent world. The deeper I go, the duller everything seems. The sun's rays struggle to reach the deeper waters and, without light, the colors disappear. With my flashlight, I can show you the true colors of the reef.

In cooler waters, the *kelp* grows thick and flows with the rhythm of the tides. In warm tropical waters, soft *coral* of many colors swells and cements itself in the currents. It is important to swim slowly and carefully across these colorful underwater gardens. A careless fin movement can destroy the fragile life. I take care not to disturb anything.

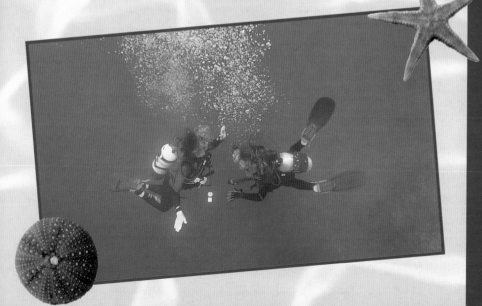

The secret of learning about the sea is to look carefully. All sorts of animals hide in, on, and under the reef. Divers who look closely may find tiny *nudibranchs*. Many people call them "butterflies of the sea." They come in just about every color combination imaginable. Don't be fooled, though; those amazing colors are not a fashion statement. They're a signal to *predators* that their bodies contain *toxins* and are not good to eat.

Nudibranchs are *carnivores*, which means they eat meat. Sometimes they even eat each other! They are also *hermaphrodites*. That means each animal is male and female at the same time.

Nudibranchs lay their eggs in clusters, which look like a rose. Some of the larger nudibranchs can lay up to one million eggs at a time!

Everywhere I look, I see something new and exciting. Nothing is what it seems. What I think are tiny colorful flowers turn out to be feathery worms. As I move closer, they sense the movement of the water and disappear within seconds, leaving nothing but a little trapdoor in the coral. They are nothing like worms that live on land.

The reef tops are covered with many beautifully shaped kelps and corals, *algae*, worms, *sponges*, and *sea squirts*. Each has its own special function. I try hard not to touch or disturb anything, but some of these squishy sponges are irresistible.

Sponges are water filters. They sift water through their bodies, capturing the nutrients they need to live. A scientist calculated that a sponge must process 1 ton of water to gain 1 ounce of body weight. That equals seven full bathtubs of water!

City beneath the Sea

Chapter Two

The sea is like a city with all its different characters. There are the solitary citizens, the roving packs, the movers and shakers, the cleaners, the slackers, and the bullies. Some of them aren't the least bit afraid of large bubble-breathing divers. The colorful clownfish, which live among the stinging arms of the anemone, seem to be fearless. If I get too close, they look at me aggressively and try to nip my fingers. I stay back and leave them to protect their territory.

There are all sorts of relationships in this underwater community. Some species have companions; others go solo. Banner fish waft through the water in pairs. They take a partner for life. I feel sad when I see one alone. It usually means it has lost its mate.

The blue cod and small blennies are the nosy neighbors in this ocean suburb. Down on the sand or perched on a rock, they rest on their *pectoral fins* and watch what's happening. I'm sure their faces show signs of disapproval.

The sandager's wrasse is much more sociable. Dressed in his striped rugby shirt, he plays a game of "now you see me, now you don't." He's checking out intruders and other males who might be competing for his harem of females. If something happens to the male sandager's wrasse, one of the dominant females in his group will quickly change sex and take over the male's role.

Other fish group together in schools.
When I look up, the surface is like a liquid
sky. Instead of airplanes, I see slivers of
silver fish swarming together. Some of these
schools will stay in one area; others will
move with the currents. There is safety in
such huge numbers. They move as a mass,
changing direction in unison, then scattering
apart when danger approaches. This is their
way of confusing predators.

Beneath the kelp
or coral, I find the
solitary citizens
of this community.
A lone scorpion fish
dressed in a coat
of many colors rests
on the reef. Some
species look exactly
like other marine life
around them. Their

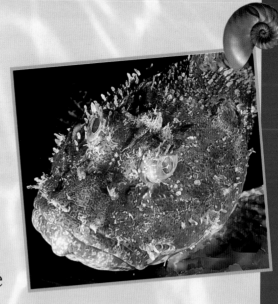

camouflage is so complete that all they need
to do is sit still and be patient. This way, they
can be the hunter and not the hunted. When
small fish swim past, the hunter snaps open
its mouth. The suction drags the prey into
the scorpion fish's cavernous mouth before
it even knows what is happening.

The lionfish belongs to the scorpion fish family. It is very beautiful, but deadly. The tips of its *dorsal spines* are poisonous. When danger approaches, the lionfish will turn its back and raise its spines. I need to be very careful not to touch any.

Some reef residents have bad reputations that they don't deserve. The needle-sharp teeth and gaping mouth of the moray eel make it look ferocious, but it is really shy. It opens and closes its mouth to keep seawater flushing across its gills. This helps it breathe. The moray eel has very poor eyesight and relies on its sense of smell to find most of its food.

Everywhere I look there are fish of every color, size, and description going about their daily business. This undersea city is a busy, bustling place.

Definitely Different

Do your folks complain that you're a messy eater? Tell them that the eating habits of the starfish are worse. Their mouths are located on the underside of their bodies. They digest their food by pouring their stomach out through their mouth. Once the food is broken down into a digestible mass, the starfish sucks it back in again!

Starfish have the ability to regenerate. This means that, if they lose a leg, they're able to grow another one. Sometimes an entire new animal can grow from the fragment that is broken off. That's why you sometimes see lopsided starfish.

Starfish belong to a family called *echinoderms*. Their bodies all have five-part symmetry and hydraulically controlled movements. That means they can use the water they live in to help their bodies move. Echinoderms come in several basic forms: sea stars, feather stars, brittle-stars, sea urchins, and sea cucumbers.

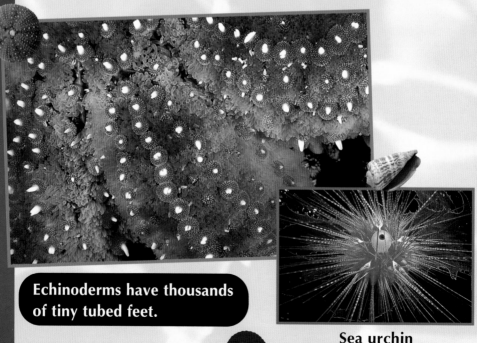

Echinoderms have thousands of tiny tubed feet.

Sea urchin

It is hard to see how these five forms are related. Take the sea cucumber: it's often difficult to tell which is the front and which is the back. Sea cucumbers are like vacuum cleaners. They move slowly along the bottom of the sea eating sand, which contains small food particles, and leaving curling trails of waste. It is safe to handle sea cucumbers, but I prefer not to. They are easily stressed and release white threads that can be as sticky as glue. Sometimes they even expel their stomach out through their mouth as a defensive measure.

Feather stars are also called *crinoids*. They don't look like starfish or sea cucumbers. They look more like flowers with many long feathery arms. Each arm is covered in hundreds of tiny hooks like Velcro. The feather star moves through the water by waving its arms, then it settles on the edge of a sponge, coral, or rock.

If I look really carefully, I may find tiny crabs or cling-fish living safely among the arms of the crinoid.

I need to be careful not to touch them. As with other starfish, their arms break off easily. This is the animal's method of getting away from danger. Luckily, they are able to grow more.

Eye Spy

While I'm watching the reef inhabitants, the reef inhabitants are watching me! Can you see that eye? It belongs to an octopus. Their eyes are very much like ours. They see us in much the same way as we see them. Because of their eyesight and well-developed brains, scientists regard them as the most intelligent *invertebrate*.

Octopuses, cuttlefish, and squid are closely related and are known as *cephalopods.* With their long tentacles, green blood, and three hearts, octopuses would look as much at home in alien movies as in our seas.

These creatures are masters of disguise. Not only can they change color and texture to match their surroundings, but, if they get extremely agitated, they can squirt a curtain of ink and magically disappear! The *siphon,* which squirts the ink, also controls the octopuses' movement. By changing the direction of the siphon and squirting water, they can propel themselves backward or forward at incredible speeds. There is no way I can keep up.

The octopus has some pretty scary relatives. There's the giant squid, which is known to grow to a length of more than 65 feet. That's longer than ten adult humans lying head to toe! The tiny blue-ringed octopus has a parrotlike beak that releases a powerful toxin. It can cause instant paralysis, and even kill a human. I'm glad it stays well hidden.

It is hard to believe that octopuses and cuttlefish are related to the creatures that live in shells. They all belong to a big group called *mollusks*. Their shells come in every shape and size you can imagine. Some, such as clams, oysters, and mussels, anchor themselves to one place and rely on their gills to filter tiny creatures from the water for their food.

Clamshells are formed by substances made in the mantle, a thin fleshy part of the clam's body located just inside the shell.

Others, such as the cowrie, move slowly across the sand at night in search of food. During the day, the animal hides beneath its hard shell. In some countries, cowrie shells were once used as money.

Empty seashells sometimes become homes for other creatures. Soft-bodied hermit crabs like nothing better than a big empty shell to move into. When the crab grows too large for a shell, it will just look around for a bigger one. Sometimes, if the shell is already inhabited, the hermit crab will try to pull the owner out of it.

Hermit crabs are *crustaceans*. Crustaceans such as crabs, crayfish, shrimps, and prawns all have a strong outer covering called an "exoskeleton." It's like a suit of armor that protects the crustaceans' internal organs and muscles. When they've grown too big for their shell, they shed it in a process called "molting." They need to stay well hidden while they wait for their new shell to harden.

Some crustaceans, such as crayfish, live in holes in the reef; others live in sandy burrows.

The blind shrimp lives in a burrow with a fish called a goby for companionship. It spends all day bulldozing out the burrow and keeping it clean while the goby, which has good eyesight, acts as a watchdog. It warns the shrimp when danger approaches.

The mantis shrimp also lives in a burrow. It is strong and cunning and attacks at lightning speed. It uses its strong claws to smash the shells of crabs, and can knock fish unconscious and pulverize worms in a fraction of a second! The blow of a large shrimp is so powerful it can break the glass of an aquarium. I think I'll keep my face mask far away from these!

Intrepid Encounters

Chapter Five

38

I know what you are going to say to me: "What about sharks?" Well, even the sharks usually mind their own business. This is their world. We are the visitors. As long as I watch and don't interfere, I shouldn't have a problem.

There are more than 350 species of sharks in the world's oceans. They are among the most sensitive of all animals. Their sense of smell is so good that some people call them "a swimming nose"! Sharks are fast, strong, and nature's waste disposal unit. They eat constantly – anything in the water is a potential dinner. There are so many small good things to eat in the sea that large aggressive animals, such as humans, are not usually on their menu.

Besides having incredibly sensitive taste, hearing, smell, and eyesight, sharks can sense minute electrical fields generated by all living organisms. That's why when a fish is in distress, a shark can often appear as if from nowhere to see what's going on.

Stingrays are basically flattened-out bottom-dwelling sharks. They're the ballerinas of the sea. They vary in size from 20 inches to 23 feet wide. Rays are no threat to humans, but they have a *venomous barb,* which I want to avoid. Sometimes they will just hover together in huge squadrons. If I'm lucky, I can float into their flying formation and hover alongside.

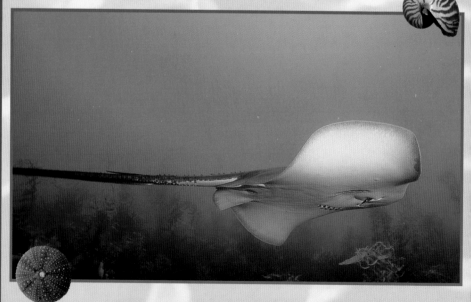

Of all the animals I have encountered, the dolphin is my favorite. The sleek powerful body of these mammals is well adapted for the underwater world. Dolphins can swim at speeds of up to 25 miles per hour, but only for a short time. Some dolphins dive to depths of almost 1,000 feet, and stay under water for up to 10 minutes. I can only dive to 100 feet safely, and no matter how hard I swim, I can never keep up. Dolphins are very intelligent. I'm sure I can see them trying to communicate with me.

To swim like a dolphin was my wildest dream. Now that I'm a diver, I've come as close as I can to making my dream a reality.

The sea and its creatures are precious. They will only survive if we care for our environment. When Jacques-Yves Cousteau, the pioneer of scuba diving, said, "The oceans of the world are ours to protect and preserve for all time," I think he was speaking to people like me.

Glossary

algae – a large group of plants without true roots, stems, and leaves, that usually grow in water

carnivore – an animal that eats meat

cephalopod – a class of active marine mollusks with a distinct head, large eyes, and a ring of tentacles around a beaked mouth

coral – a substance secreted by certain marine organisms that hardens into a limestone skeleton

crinoid – a class of the echinoderm phylum that includes feather stars and sea lilies

crustacean – a large group of animals with hard external skeletons and many jointed legs

dorsal spine – a spine running along the back of a fish

echinoderm – a group of sea creatures that includes sea eggs, starfish, crinoids, and sea cucumbers

hermaphrodite – an animal that possesses both male and female reproductive organs

invertebrate – an animal without a backbone. This classification includes all animals except mammals, birds, reptiles, amphibians, eels, and fish.

kelp – a large brown seaweed

mollusk – an invertebrate that has a soft unsegmented body and, often, a hard shell. This classification includes snails, slugs, bivalves, squid, and octopuses.

nudibranch – a shell-less sea slug

pectoral fin – a fin that extends from just behind the head of a fish or whale

predator – an animal that survives by eating other animals

sea squirt – an aquatic animal with a rubbery baglike body through which water flows in and out

siphon – a tubelike organ in an aquatic animal for drawing in and expelling liquid

sponge – an aquatic animal with a porous body and a rigid or elastic external skeleton

toxin – a poison

venomous barb – a sharp poisonous extension

From the Author

I have always wanted to share the amazing underwater world with a young person. There are many books written about marine creatures, but I wanted to write a nonfiction book that was not only full of interesting information, but written in the voice of a young person. I suggested the idea to my best friend's daughter, Samantha. She couldn't wait to get started! Samantha often felt seasick as we traveled by boat to different dive sites, but once in the water she swam as naturally as a fish.

You might never have the chance to dive, but if you have followed Samantha on this adventure, I will have been able to share some of the magic of the ocean with you.

Angie Belcher

When I first saw the beautiful colors and life under the waves, I knew I had to take photos of it to share with the rest of the world.

Taking underwater photographs is not easy. First, you must become an excellent diver. Then you must learn how to take great photos. There is a lot to think about. I have to make sure I don't kick up sand, break coral, or scare away animals with my bubbles. I also need to keep an eye on how deep I am, how much air I am using, and how long I have been under water.

Diving with Samantha was a real pleasure because she was so enthusiastic and learned so quickly. I couldn't talk to her under water, so after each dive we would discuss what had happened and how we could improve the photos by changing her body position, making eye contact with marine creatures, and paying attention to the photographer at all times.

Andy Belcher

If you have enjoyed reading *Samantha's Sea*, read these other *Storyteller* Chapter Books.

Wolfmaster

Aunt Victoria's Monster

Survival in Cyberspace

A Friend in the Wild

Groovy Gran and the Karaoke Kid

Cat Culture

Cheetah Conservation